John Leighton, Robert Hall Baynes, E.F.C Clarke

Autumn Memories and Other Verses

John Leighton, Robert Hall Baynes, E.F.C Clarke

Autumn Memories and Other Verses

ISBN/EAN: 9783337375331

Printed in Europe, USA, Canada, Australia, Japan

Cover: Foto ©Andreas Hilbeck / pixelio.de

More available books at **www.hansebooks.com**

AUTUMN MEMORIES

AND

OTHER VERSES

BY THE VICAR OF

S. MICHAEL AND ALL ANGELS, COVENTRY

WITH TEN ILLUSTRATIONS BY

JOHN LEIGHTON, F.S.A., AND E. F. C. CLARKE

THIRD THOUSAND

LONDON

HOULSTON AND WRIGHT

65, PATERNOSTER ROW

MDCCCLXIX.

✠

TO THE

Countess of Aylesford,

THE FOLLOWING VERSES,

WITH MUCH REGARD,

AND BY HER LADYSHIP'S KIND PERMISSION,

Are Inscribed.

✠

PREFATORY NOTE.

I HAVE been asked more than once to collect together the few Verses and Hymns that are found in this little Volume. Some of them have found their way into many of our Church Hymnals, and others have ministered consolation and solace to weary and sorrowing hearts.

The fact that the first edition has been exhausted in the space of a few weeks is a gratifying proof that the request of my friends was not altogether unreasonable.

That these Hymns may continue to be of service to the Church Militant here upon earth is my highest wish, as it must ever be my fullest reward.

R. H. B.

Easter, MDCCCLXIX

CONTENTS.

CONTENTS.

Autumn Memories.

I.

BY THE LAKE.

HEMMED in by mountains, girdled with
    dark pines,
    The lake lay sleeping; not a ruffle stirred
Its deep, calm waters, and the lengthening
    lines
    Of shadow kissed its breast: no sound
    was heard.

Above, the clouds were coursing through
    the sky,
    Save where there gleamed a deep of
    purest blue;
And one star, like a signal lamp on high,
    Into a form of wondrous beauty grew.

It sparkled clear, like that strange Star of
    old
    That led the wise men o'er their weary
    way,
Till they had brought their frankincense and gold,
And worshipped where the world's Redeemer lay.

I stood beside the margin ; 'twas a sea
  Of glass ; faint ripples dreamed along the shore :
I wondered if more beautiful could be
  The Land where seas and stars shall be no more.

And then I thought me of that lake of old
  Where once the Master 'mid the darkness trod,
And at His word the angry billows rolled
  Their foam into a calm, and owned their God.

Then o'er me came faint glimpses of a stream
  Whose waves make glad the City up above ;
Lit up for ever by the sunny gleam,
  Reflecting only heavenly light and love.

Oh, when the storms of life have ceased to beat,
  Safe to the haven where we all would be,
Lord Jesu, bring our worn and wandering feet,
  Beside the margin of the Crystal Sea.

II.

IN THE CLOISTERS.

ARD by the lake, girt with its forest zone,
　　The Abbey stands,—relic of days' gone
　　　by :
The ivy clambers o'er the crumbling stone,
　　And mosses sleep where the dead calmly
　　　lie.

Amid the ruins, o'er the chancel floor,
　　The dank weeds thicken, and the rains
　　　descend ;
The choir of voices sweet is heard no more,
　　Nor to the altar priests their footsteps
　　　wend.

But memories cluster round the chapel grey,
　　And, lingering there, we live the past again,
And seem to hear, adown the lonely way,
　　The priestly footfall, and the solemn strain.

Still falls the yew tree's shadow on the aisle,
　　Wearing its crown of life amid decay ;
Catching in early morn the sun's warm smile,
　　Watching the stars gleam till the break of day.

Wait a few years, and that dark yew shall fade :
　　But the true-hearted in their cloistered bed
Shall wake to life immortal, and, arrayed
　　In robes of white, safe to their home be led.

That home, the Temple time can never dim ;—
　　No shadows frown, and no sad tears are there.
Oh, at the last, to join that ceaseless hymn,
　　The crown of all His perfected to wear !

III.

AMONG THE RUINS.

QUIET autumn eve. The sun was flinging
   Long deepening shadows on the purple
    hill ;
And, save the vespers happy birds were
    singing,
   Or the faint sheep-bell, all was hushed
    and still.

The spot was sacred,—ruined arch and
    column,
   The traceried window, and the altar-stair,
Told of a worship, catholic and solemn,
   That in the ages gone was offered there.

But now the porch, o'ergrown with weeds
    and grasses,
   Leads only to the crumbling aisle and
    nave ;
Along the groinèd roof the stray bat passes,
   While through the transepts winter tempests rave.

But 'mid the ruins, all unmarred and stately,
   A large stone Cross lifted its solemn head ;
The steps were worn, and the sight moved me greatly;
   It seemed to speak of Life amongst the dead.

Emblem and shadow of a truth still deeper,—
    He who in Christ's dear Cross hath healing found,
Shall safe be garnered by the Angel Reaper,
    And stand secure upon the Holy Ground.

O Christ, the merciful High Priest and holy,
    Keep Thou these hearts from desolation free ;
And from their inner shrine, made pure and lowly,
    Let worship rise like incense up to Thee.

Cleanse them from earthly dross, Thou true Refiner,
    Thy living light upon their dimness pour ;
Until we see Thee in the land diviner,
    And with the Angels tread the Golden Floor.

IV.

AT SEA.

ROBED like a king, with coronet of gold,
    Grandly the sun went down beneath the
      sea,
Flushing the waves with amber as they
    rolled,
    And opening up the deeps of heaven to
      me.

Around,—the waste of waters, the white
    foam
    Gathering in snowy flakes and glittering
      spray ;
Above,—the clouds, like great cathedral
    dome,
    All tinted with the hues of dying day.

Yet this vast ocean, with its restless tides,
    He holdeth in the hollow of His hand ;
The clouds, the chariot where His glory rides,
    And but His footstool all the peopled land !

O Might and Majesty ! all thought above !
    How eloquent these billows are of Thee !
O depth untold ! O mystery of love,
    To know that outstretched Hand was pierced for me !

BY THE SHORE

HE sun had set in glory; clouds of gold
   Were fringed with wondrous purple;
    crimson bars
Reddened the foaming billows as they
    rolled,
   Till from heaven's blue gleamed out the
    silent stars.

Then passed the Moon up to her queenly
    throne,
   The waters flashed with gems and glit-
    tering ore ;
All earth was hushed to stillness, save the
    moan
    Of the monotonous waves along the
    shore.

I watched the strange clouds as they floated by,
   Some dark and murky, with a threatening glare ;
Some white and fleecy mounting up the sky,
   Like veilèd angels on a shadowy stair.

And while I gazed I wondered what might be
   The new, diviner Land for which we wait ;
For earth itself, from stain of evil free,
   Would gleam with glory from the Golden Gate.

But there no clouds shall gather, and no more
   The ocean rage—emblem of deep unrest ;
No storms shall sweep across that radiant shore,
   No night shall shroud that City of the blest !

This earth is beautiful ; o'er land and sea
   The mighty shadow of God's thought is cast ;
But brighter far the Home that is to be,—
   O Christ ! receive us to that Home at last !

S. MICHAEL'S, COVENTRY.

"Dugdale mentions this church as being first named in the time of King Stephen, who came to the throne in 1135 A.D., and in whose reign it was given, by the name of the Chapel of S. Michael, to the monks of Coventry by Ranulph, Earl of Chester. The tower was commenced in 1373, and completed in 1394.

"The tower and spire of S. Michael's Church, taken together, present one of the finest examples of Early Perpendicular architecture, and of the steeples which rise from the ground it has no superior in England, taking its height in proportion to its base. Salisbury and Norwich steeples are higher, but their height is less apparent, from the great breadth of base from which they rise. The entire height of tower and spire is 303 feet; the length of the church is 303 feet, and the greatest breadth 127. The interior of this majestic structure, which is the largest parish church in England, consists of nave, chancel, and four aisles. The long lines of tall and graceful columns, supporting arches of vast span, together with the noble range of venerable clerestory windows and the fine oaken-ribbed roof, form a glorious and impressive piece of church scenery."—*Taunton's "History of Coventry,"* pp. 131, 134.

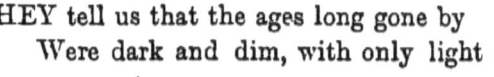HEY tell us that the ages long gone by
    Were dark and dim, with only light of
        stars ;
  That truth and freedom were but left to
        die
    Within strong prison bars.

It may be so ; and yet, for loftiest thought,
  For rare self-sacrifice and plenteous gold,
With willing hearts for God's high service
        brought,
    They were brave days of old.

CHURCH OF S. MICHAEL AND ALL ANGELS, COVENTRY.

Look at this glorious building ! how it stands
   Midway 'twixt earth and heaven ; a stately pile,
Where Faith may worship with uplifted hands
      Within its solemn aisle.

I gaze at early morning, when the light
   Streams through the eastern windows, strong and fair,
Scattering its coloured glories, wondrous bright,
      Along the marble stair.

I gaze at noontide, when the golden glow
   Flushes with life each arch and column high :
I rest beneath its shadow, and I know
      It makes Heaven seem more nigh ;

At even, when the moonbeams, cold and clear,
   Strew with weird phantoms all the silent floor ;
And in the stillness nave and aisle appear
      More marvellous than before.

O wealth of beauty ! joy perpetual !
   Vision of splendour ! with thy shadowy Spire,
Meet type and emblem of the jasper wall,
      And of the heavenly Choir.

Fair temple of our God ! long may'st thou stand,
   The shrine of Jesus, storehouse of His grace,
Until we reach the bright and perfect Land,
      And see Him face to face.

IN MEMORIAM.

BONCHURCH.

13th Sunday after Trinity, MDCCCLXIII.

NEVER can forget that Sunday night,
  I sat alone beside the burial sod,
I watched the moon sail o'er her sea of light,
    And the dear stars of God.

No sound disturbed the stillness of that time,
  Save the low murmur of the restless wave,
A seeming echo to the Church bell's chime,
    Beside that cross-crowned grave.

I thought of those whose struggles all were
      o'er
    In the calm rest of God's untroubled
      sleep ;
Of white-robed saints upon the tideless shore,
  Where none may toil or weep.

And then I thought of that far better Land,
  From every storm and darkening tempest free,
Where never billow sobs upon the strand,
    For *there* is no more sea.

Until I almost longed to be at rest
  From life's exceeding sorrow and its care ;
To join, e'en now, the anthems of the blest,
    Their perfect gladness share.

But while I dreamed of God's eternal Home,
  Watching the shadows as they flitted by,
Voices all dear and earnest seemed to come
    From out the grave and sky,

Bidding me work while it is called To-day ;
  To suffer, if He will, and so be strong ;
To use His blessed gifts as best I may,
    For no true life is long.

Thus, from this lonely tomb beside the shore,
  I learnt the lesson,—hardest yet the best ; —
I will be patient—I will dream no more,
    And *He* will give me rest.

FOR I KNOW THEIR SORROWS.

WHEN across the heart deep waves of sorrow
  Break, as on a dry and barren shore ;
When Hope glistens with no bright to-
    morrow,
  And the storm seems sweeping evermore ;

When the cup of every earthly gladness
  Bears no taste of the life-giving stream,
And high hopes, as though to mock our
    sadness,
  Fade and die as in some fitful dream :

Who shall hush the weary spirit's chiding,
  Who the aching void within shall fill ?
Who shall whisper of a peace abiding,
  And each surging billow calmly still ?

Only He whose wounded heart was broken
  With the bitter Cross and thorny Crown,
Whose dear love glad words of joy had spoken,
  Who His life for us laid meekly down.

Blessed Healer ! all our burdens lighten ;
  Give us Peace, Thine own sweet Peace, we pray ;
Keep us near Thee till the Morn shall brighten,
  And all mists and shadows flee away !

LENT.

OW long and deep the shadows of our Lent,
  Flung o'er its penitential forty days,
With here and there a ray of sunshine sent
  From Sunday's gladness and its burst of
    praise!

Our sins and sorrows, like some surging tide,
  Wave after wave, beat o'er our struggling
    life,
The deeds of darkness that we fain would
    hide—
  The broken vow, the fainting in the strife.

Helpless and sad, O Christ, we come to
    Thee!
  Thou for our sake wast to the desert led,
Unharmed didst cross temptation's stormy
    sea,
  That we, Thy children, might be comforted.

In all points tempted, e'en as we are now,
  O Man Divine! like to Thy brethren made,
The thorny crown girdled Thy sacred Brow,
  That weary hearts might look to Thee for aid.

Thy cross, upreared on Calvary's altar high,
    The nail-print, and the Side so rudely riven,
The mid-day darkness and the piercing cry,
    Tell the glad story of our sin forgiven.

Thus to our hearts the long, long gloom of Lent,
    Leading us on to Easter's brightest glow,
Becomes a living type and sacrament
    Of all God's discipline of love below.

The bitter first, and then the endless sweet,
    The hard, rough way, and then the golden floor,
The fiery furnace, then nor sun nor heat,
    The Cross, and then the Crown for evermore !

THEY SHALL LOOK UPON ME WHOM THEY HAVE PIERCED.

(A FRAGMENT.)

SALEM! for thy long drear night of woe,
What tears of bitterest grief might justly
 flow!
But though at morning's dawn and even-
 ing's close
Thy wandering children find no sweet
 repose—
Though exiled now, 'mid many an alien
 throng
Scattered and lone—a byword and a song—
Though Israel be not gathered,* and the
 cry
Of " Allah " rises proudly to the sky,
As still at eventide those massive stones
Send a sad echo to their yearning moans:
Fear not, O Sion! wipe thy tearful eyes—
Shake off thy bands, and from the dust arise!
Thy dead shall live—the bones all dry and pale,†
With moving myriads shall fill the vale;

---

* Isa. xlix. 5.   † Isa. xxvi. 19.

c

For those few tombs that now bestrew the sod,
So shall thy seed be, as the stars of God !
E'en now the gloomy shadows flee away,
And Faith exulting waits the break of day !

I know not if the visions glimpsed of old,
In glowing strains by gifted prophets told,
Shall find their full fruition 'neath a sky
Where sorrow reigns, and all are born to die !
Nor if on Sion's summit e'er again
Shall rise the turrets of a statelier fane ;
And, brought to their ancestral home once more,
Ephraim and Judah, side by side, adore :
But this I know—o'er all their darkened sight
Their God shall pour a flood of holiest light :
They shall behold—and as they gaze shall mourn*—
The spotless Lamb who all "their griefs hath borne ; "
Before His Cross—the true Messiah—fall ;
The Man of Sorrows—yet the Lord of all !

And this I know—in Sion's fairer shrine,
From Eden's ruins reared, by power Divine,
As precious stones they shall for ever stand,
'Mid jewels garnered by no mortal Hand.
E'en now Heaven's azure portals wide unfold ;
I catch the echoing strains from harps of gold :
Nearest the Throne, with blaze of glory dim,
Thy sons, O Judah, chant the loftiest hymn !
And Israel's ransomed multitudes are seen
Casting their crowns before the " Nazarene."

* Zech. xii. 10.

GOOD FRIDAY.

DAY of sorrow, deeper than our thought,
  When Christ our Passover for us was
      slain,
When He with price of Blood our pardon
      bought,
    His loss our endless gain.

O Day of woe, and unknown agony,
  When by the margin of the shadowy
      dead,
The Christ sent up that bitter, sweetest cry,
    Lo, " It is finishèd !"

Yet Day of solemn Joy art thou to me,
  For to Thy healing Cross, I, weary, bring
My heart's sad tale of sin and misery,
    And to that Cross I cling.

I know that there my heaviest sin was borne
  By sin's Atoner, Human yet Divine ;
I see the wounded Side all pierced and torn,
    And know the spear was mine.

I trace the print of nails in hands and feet,
   The Crown of thorns purpling Thy sacred brow,
And I can almost feel my hard heart beat
     Beneath Thy sorrow now !

I yearn for Rest, but o'er Life's stormy wave
   No Rest I find, save 'neath Thy shelter true ;
Here is the Haven, here the peace I crave,
     That maketh all things new.

Thy Cross shall teach me all the deeps of sin
   That to Thy mighty sufferings brought Thee down ;
Thy death, eternal Life for me shall win,
     That Cross, a glorious Crown.

Thy fellowship of suffering here below,
   Thy patient love, O dying Christ, be mine !
Then give me all Thy Easter joy to know,
     And in Thy Likeness shine !

THE HOLY COMMUNION.

AS o'er life's dangerous paths we sadly tread,
　While passing through this strange and
　　　weary land,
　Lo! a rich Feast of Love for us is spread
　　By the nail-piercèd Hand.

Fainting and footsore, toil we in the way;
　No manna glistens on the desert sod;
And yet to earnest souls, that kneel and
　　　pray,
　There comes the Bread of God.

For us there flows no pure life-giving rill,
　Such as for Israel's need of old sufficed;
Yet here our thirsting spirits we may fill
　　With the glad Wine of Christ.

Resting beneath His shadow, cool and sweet,
　We gain fresh strength for conflict with our foes
Here the lone desert, with its sultry heat,
　　Doth blossom as the rose.

And though these earthly shadows, dark and dim,
　Veil from our sight His blessed Presence now,
Yet Faith exulting lifts her eyes to Him,
　　And sees the thorn-crowned Brow!

Waves from the ocean of His mighty love
    Break in rejoicing on the expectant shore,
Whispering sweet voices of the Land above,
      Where storms shall be no more.

Glad, then, and sacred to all lowly hearts,
    The Table spread by the dear Hands of Christ,
Where He His gifts of blessing still imparts
      In Holy Eucharist !

Telling of Calvary and its bitter Cross,
    The nails, the thorns, and the spear-wounded Side ;
Bidding us count all earthly things but loss
      For love of Him who died.

Pointing us onward to the Day of Light,
    When, 'mid the glories of His Home Divine,
Christ and His Church, in robes of purest white,
      Shall drink His own new Wine !

"MY FLESH IS MEAT INDEED, AND MY BLOOD IS DRINK INDEED."

REAT Shepherd of Thy ransomed Flock,
  Send down on all Thy gifts to-day,—
The water from the riven Rock,
  The manna gleaming on our way.

Yea, more ! from out Thy pierced side,
  Whence flowed the Water and the Blood,
Pour on our souls the crimson tide,
  And wash us in that cleansing flood.

Still journeying on amid the waste,
  And fainting oft beneath the strife,
Our longing spirits yearn to taste
  Thy heavenly food, O Bread of Life !

And when our broken cisterns fail,
  And leave us thirsting on the sod ;
When all the powers of sin assail,
  We need Thy strength, O Wine of God !

Come to each waiting heart, O Christ !
  In all the fulness of Thy love ;
Make now this blessed Eucharist
  The earnest of Thy joys above.   AMEN.

EASTER.

S Spring's sweet breath after long wintry
    snow,
As land to voyager o'er pathless sea,
As daybreak after weary night of woe,
    Is Easter joy to me !

All Lenten shadows over ! and the light
Around us and within so sweet and strong,
Teach us, O risen Master, how aright
    To sing our Easter song.

We stand to-day beside Thy open tomb,
We gaze on "linen clothes" with reverent
    heed,
And hear the angels whispering through
    the gloom,
    "Not here—but risen indeed !"

And all the story of Thy love divine
Throbs through our hearts, longing, O Christ, for Thee.
The bitter chalice, with the deadly wine,
    Was drained to set us free.

The grave is dark no more! a stream of light
He, rising, left behind for all His own.
Death's chain is broken by His arm of might,
 And rolled away the stone.

Now Easter-light flushes the morning sky,
Thy Form we see, all changed, and yet the same.
Master! we kneel before Thee; hear our cry,
 And call us each by name.*

When evening shadows lengthen all around,
And we to Emmaus take our weary way,
With us, O risen Saviour, still be found,
 And turn our night to day.

And from Thy radiant throne of light above,
Oh, send us, till our desert wanderings cease,
Thine own best legacy of tender love,
 Thy sweetest gift of peace!

Then, at the last, when all shall wake who sleep,
Made like to Thee, in raiment white and fair,
Oh, bid us welcome to Thy home, to keep
 Our endless Easter there!

---

* "Jesus saith unto her, Mary."—S. JOHN xx. 16.

THE LORD'S SUPPER.

" To know the love of Christ, which passeth knowledge."

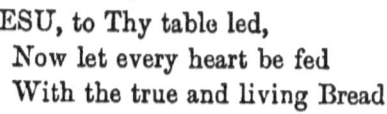

ESU, to Thy table led,
　Now let every heart be fed
　With the true and living Bread.

While in penitence we kneel,
Thy sweet Presence let us feel,
All Thy wondrous love reveal!

While on Thy dear Cross we gaze,
Mourning o'er our sinful ways,
Turn our sadness into praise!

When we taste the mystic Wine,
Of Thine outpoured blood the sign,
Fill our hearts with Love Divine!

Draw us to Thy wounded side,
Whence there flowed the healing tide;
There our sins and sorrows hide!

From the bonds of sin release,
Cold and wavering faith increase,
Lamb of God, grant us Thy peace!

Lead us by Thy piercèd Hand,
Till around Thy Throne we stand,
In the bright and better land!　AMEN.

"AND WHEN THEY HAD SUNG AN HYMN,
THEY WENT OUT UNTO THE MOUNT
OF OLIVES."

CALM lay the city in its double sleep,
    Beneath the Paschal Moon's cold, silvery
        light,
That flung broad shadows o'er the rugged
        steep
    Of Olivet that night.

But soon the calm was broken, and the
        sound
    Of strains all sweet and plaintive filled
        the air ;
And deep-toned voices echoing all around,
    Made music everywhere.

The Holy Rite is o'er ; the Blessed Sign
    Is given to cheer us in this earthly strife ;
The Bread is broken, and outpoured the
        Wine,—
    Symbol of better Life.

The bitter cup of wrath before Him lies ;
    And yet as up the steep they pass along,
The mighty Victim to the Sacrifice,
    They cheer the way with song.

We ne'er can know such sorrow as that night
   Pierced to the heart the suffering Son of God ;
And every earthly sadness is but light
   To that dark path He trod !

And yet how faint and feeble rise our songs ;
   How oft we linger 'mid the shadows dim ;
Nor give the glory that to Him belongs
   In Eucharistic hymn !

O for an echo of that chant of praise ;
   O for a voice to sing His mighty love ;
O for a refrain of the hymns they raise
   In the bright Home above !

Touch Thou our wayward hearts, and let them be
   In stronger faith to Thy glad service given,
Till, o'er the margin of Time's surging sea,
   We sing the song of Heaven !

THE EARLY SACRAMENT.

WAS early morning, in the winter-time,
  The sun just struggling through dark
    rifts of cloud;
  The air was filled with music, sweet and
    loud,
That echoed from the church-bells' pealing
    chime.

I entered quietly by chancel door;
  More dear than ever did the old Church
    seem,
  Like vision faint of Heaven discerned
    in dream.
Deep shadows lingered on the marble floor;

While from each window, with its golden glow,
  Some blessed story of the Gospel shone,
  Bidding each weary pilgrim journey on
To that Bright Land they all at last shall know.

The Feast was ready, and the Table spread
  With heavenly Food, in presence of our Foes;
  There for the faint the Cup that overflows,
And for the hungry soul the living Bread.

I knelt before His Table, longing there
 Deep draughts to drink from out Salvation's well ;
 Praying the Christ within my heart to dwell,
And make it evermore His temple fair !

And as I knelt, a gladness o'er me came,
 Not all of earth, but calm, and full of rest ;
 And, like St. John upon the Saviour's breast,
I felt the sweetness of that blessed Name.

O Feast of love and solace ! what they lose
 Who turn away from Banquet so divine !
 Who leave untasted Heaven's most strengthening Wine
And Manna !—God's own Bread from Heaven refuse !

SUNDAY EVENING. .

 IS Sunday Eve in summer's sweetest time,
   The sun just sinking 'neath the purple
     hills,
   A strange, husht calm my inmost spirit
     fills,
As here I listen to the old church-chime.

Before me, like the glassy sea of old—
   Waveless in Sabbath-quiet sleeps the
     bay,
   One white sail glimmering in the far-
     away,
Amid the waters tinged with dying gold.

Gently the twilight shadows all the land,
   While from the ghostly clouds that
     fringe the sky,
   The moon all pale and new gleams forth on high,
Like silver sickle held by Angel-hand.

Surely all nature owns the Sabbath hour,
   Else why this peace so sweetly hovering round,
   This silence, eloquent, yet so profound,
That holds us in its deep, mysterious power ?

O Evening flusht with gladness! how I love
   Thy peaceful benediction! like the dew
   Baptizing earth, and making all things new,
Thou liftest lower thoughts and hopes above!

I think of Eden and its sinless bowers,
   Of God Himself walking in cool of day,
   Where yet no trail of deadly serpent lay,
And gladdening Adam through the restful hours.

I think of Joseph's garden, and its cave
   Rock-hewn, from whence the mighty Conqueror rose
   The Lord of Life, who vanquished all our foes,
And flung a ray of brightness o'er the grave!

But most I think me of that sunlit Shore,
   Where tempests beat not, and no shadows fall,
   Where God and His dear love are all-in-all,
And we shall falter, sin, and weep no more.

That Rest remaineth; yet these days of peace
   Are foretastes sweet of that glad Home above,
   Where all His perfected in light and love
At last shall meet, and every sigh shall cease.

Lord of the Sabbath! Whom our hearts adore,
   Accept the feeble anthem of our praise,
   And fit us holier, loftier hymns to raise
In Thy great Temple—blest for evermore!

THE QUEEN'S ACCESSION.

JUNE 20.

" Let Her always possess the hearts of Her People, that they may never be wanting in honour to Her Person, and dutiful submission to Her Authority : let Her Reign be long and prosperous, and crown Her with Immortality in the Life to come : Through Jesus Christ our Lord—AMEN."

RING out the merry peals from every steeple,
 Fling wide the Church's doors for prayer
 and praise,
With thankful hearts let loyal Priest and
 People
 Their joyful Anthems raise.

Thou King of Kings, Who in Thy mercy
 carest
For all Mankind, and callest them Thine
 own,
We pray Thee send Thy Blessing, rich and
 rarest,
 On England and her Throne.

But most we pray Thee, on this day of
 gladness,
To pour Thy light where darkest clouds have been ;
Turn into joy each trace of lingering sadness,
 And bless our noble Queen.

D

Long years have passed since her young brow, so tender,
   The weight of England's jewelled crown first bore,
And the one prayer went up, "O God, defend Her,
      And guard Her evermore !"

And all those years, Her one and high endeavour
   Has only been to do, and live, the right ;
This jewel on her Coronet, for ever,
      Will gleam with purest light.

No Sun on Her dominions ever setteth,
   But stronger than Her power by land or sea,
Her People's constant love that ne'er forgetteth
      To think, O Queen, of Thee !

And though the shadow of a life-long sorrow
   Still stays beside Thee, soon shall dawn the day
When God's dear Hand, in His own bright to-morrow,
      Shall wipe all tears away.

God bless Thee, noble Lady—and all voices
   Now blend in one great Litany of prayer,
To-day our Land through all its coasts rejoices,
      Thy Queenly rule to bear.

Long may'st Thou reign in gentle love and duty,
   And when Thou lay'st Thine earthly Sceptre down,
Behold the King of Kings in all His beauty,
      And wear Heaven's fadeless Crown.

A VISION OF THE CRUSADES.

'WAS twilight's soothing hour; around
    there lay
A calm responsive to the dying day.
The winds had sunk athwart the moaning
    deep,
And wearied eyes were lulled in welcome
    sleep.
Within the cypress grove whose shadows
    wave
In mournful silence o'er a monarch's
    grave,*
Methought I lay. No sound disturbed
    the air ;
All Nature's voice seemed hushed in
    silent prayer.
The Moslem turrets, through the starry night,
Shone coldly fair, in lines of silver light.
Sad memories, as I caught their tapering forms,
Came rushing o'er me, quick as summer storms.
Now bright, now dark, the spectral fancies crowd,
Like April sunshine struggling through the cloud :

---

* "Tradition says that Solomon was buried on Mount Zion."—
Bannister's "*Holy Land,*" p. 298.

Zion's proud daughters, mincing as they go—
Anon her sons led captive by the foe ;
The harp and viol, that mirthful music made—
That harp unstrung beneath the willow shade ;
In holy place, as long by seers foretold,
The hateful desolation standing bold.
Assyrian, Roman, Moslem guard the wall ;
By turns they triumph, and by turns they fall.

Thus, while I muse, sweet slumber seals mine eyes,
And glorious visions of the past arise.
No more alone, but with a mighty band,
With sword and helmet armed for fight, I stand.
The red-cross banner flutters in the winds ;
One stern resolve those gathered myriads binds—
From proud usurpers' faithless grasp to wrest
That sacred mount Jehovah loveth best.
And theirs the task to conquer or to die ;
The martyr crown, or palm of victory.

'Tis early morn ; the hills are fringed with gold,
When Salem's towers their eager eyes behold.
Then sudden, as with one strange impulse stirred,
That stalwart host is still, nor voice is heard ;
And princely warriors, with their vassal train,
The mitred abbot, and the hermit plain,
All lowly bending, kiss the hallowed sod
That felt the footprint of the Son of God.
Then on in haste, with gleaming armour bright,
And hearts undaunted, to the fearful fight.

Bravely the aliens guard the steep, and well,
Their glances flashing with the rage of hell :
Thrice they repulse the Christians, while around
The dead, the dying, thickly strew the ground,
'Mid storms of arrows rattling on their mail,
Their well-tried strength begins at last to fail,
When lo ! on yonder mountain's lofty crest,
With red Cross flaming on his girded breast,
An angel-form, bright as the noontide ray,
Bids the brave Godfrey once more lead the fray ;
Beckons him on with radiant hand divine—
And quick his throbbing heart obeys the sign.
One deadlier conflict still, and all is o'er ;
The Moslem soldier treads the heights no more !
At that same hour, when Calvary's darkened steep*
Was rocked with echoing thunder, loud and deep,
What time the Lord of life a Victim lay
Nailed to the tree, and breathed His soul away—
On Zion's hill the faithful warriors rest,
And plant their standard on its yielding breast.

O wondrous change ! the temple arches wide
Echo glad anthems to the Crucified :
Before that altar rises once again
The sacred symbol of His bitter pain ;
The chant of praise with adoration blends,
And incense pure from lowly hearts ascends.

---

* "The City was taken on Friday afternoon, at three o'clock."—
Williams' " Holy City."

Gone is the spell; the dream has died away;
It told of better things, too bright to stay.
'Twas but a ray of sunshine through the gloom—
A Christian requiem sung o'er Israel's tomb.
The vanquished alien soon regains his spoil,
And drives his conquerors from the hallowed soil;
'Mid weeping maids, with trailing garments torn,
The holy Rood with taunting jest is borne,
And from the summit of that temple fair
Fresh floats the golden Crescent on the air.

CHANCEL OF S. MICHAEL AND ALL ANGELS, COVENTRY.

CONFIRMATION.

"Promise unto the Lord your God, and keep it."

OLY Spirit, Lord of glory,
  Look on us, Thy flock, to-day,
Meekly kneeling at Thine altar,
  For Thy sevenfold gifts we pray;
Guide us all our earthly journey
  In the true and narrow way.

Foes on every hand are round us,
  And our hearts are weak and frail;
Gird us with Thy heavenly armour,
  Never let us yield or quail;
Give us victory in the struggle
  When the hosts of sin assail.

Blessed Jesu! draw Thou near us,
  As before Thy Cross we bow,
Help us to be true and faithful,
  Seal our sacramental vow;
We Thy soldiers are and servants,
  Hear our solemn promise now!

Lead us by Thy Hand so piercèd,
　　Through the waste, with evil rife,
Feed us with the Heavenly Manna,
　　That we faint not in the strife ;
Slake our weary spirits thirsting
　　With the Wine of endless Life.

Looking ever unto Jesus,
　　Leaning on His staff and rod,
May we follow in His footsteps,
　　Tread the path that Jesus trod ;
Till we dwell with Him for ever
　　In the Paradise of God !—AMEN.

"*HE ASKED LIFE OF THEE, AND THOU GAVEST HIM A LONG LIFE, EVEN FOR EVER AND EVER.*"

"HE is not dead," but only lieth sleeping
    In the sweet refuge of his Master's
      Breast,
    And far away from sorrow, toil, and
      weeping,
      "He is not dead," but only taking
      rest.

What though the highest hopes he
    dearly cherished,
    All faded gently as the setting sun;
What though our own fond expectations
    perished,
    Ere yet life's noblest labour seemed
    begun;

What though he standeth at no earthly
    altar,—
Yet in white raiment, on the golden floor,
Where love is perfect and no step can falter,
He serveth as a Priest for evermore!

O glorious end of life's short day of sadness!
  O blessed course so well and nobly run!
O home of true and everlasting gladness!
  O crown unfading! and so early won!

Though tears will fall, we bless Thee, O our Father,
  For the dear One for ever with the blest,
And wait the Easter dawn when Thou shalt gather
  Thine own, long parted, to their endless rest.

"*THE SEA OF GLASS, MINGLED WITH FIRE.*"

 SEA of glass,—calm, infinite depths of
    ocean,
  Across whose shoreless waves no tempests
    beat,
Nor heaving billows in their wild commotion
  . Foam out their angry heat.

O vision fair, O mystery of wonder,
  Sure type of heaven's unbroken harmony,
The wave and flame no longer kept
    asunder,
  Fire mingles with the sea !

The fire of endless love—the full reflection
  Of the great sunlight of the Master's
    face,
And all the children of the Resurrection
  Held in His sweet embrace !

Far on that sea in beauty all-excelling,
  Firm as those waves of old that Jesus trod,
The white-robed saints, glad songs of triumph swelling,
  Stand with the harps of God.

O but to catch, amid some dream-like slumber,
    Faint echoes of that anthem deep and high,
Sung by the multitude no man can number
    Beneath that cloudless sky !

Hush ! like the distant sound of billows roaring,
    Or booming of the thunder far away,
I hear the strain that floats from saints adoring
    Amid that perfect day.

'Tis the same song oft sung by faltering voices
    Of pilgrims weary, with their bleeding feet ;
That now the ransomed host for aye rejoices
    Upon the golden street.

Worthy the Lamb ! we sing it in our sadness,
    As to His cross we cling, that cross we love ;
Worthy the Lamb ! they chant with endless gladness
    In the bright choir above.

O song of songs ! all other far exceeding,
    Full of His love, unfathomed and unpriced,
That tells us of the suffering, dying, bleeding,
    And ever-living Christ !

Upon that sea of glass, all storms passed o'er us,
    With the whole Church before the great I AM,
O may I join that everlasting chorus
    Of Moses and the Lamb !

THEN THE DEVIL LEAVETH HIM AND
BEHOLD ANGELS CAME AND MINISTERED VNTO HIM

THE FIRST SUNDAY IN LENT.

"Then was Jesus led up of the Spirit into the wilderness to be tempted of the devil."—S. Matt. iv. 1.

"Then the devil leaveth Him, and, behold, angels came and ministered unto Him."—S. Matt. iv. 11.

P, from the fresh and pure Baptismal wave,
　Where lingered yet the shadow of the
　　Dove ;
Up, from the echo of that Voice which gave
　The sweet assurance of His Father's love ;

Into the desert-waste, so lone and drear,
　Whose burning sands no mark of foot-
　　prints bore,
And the weird silence of the rock and mere
　Was startled only by the wild beasts' roar.*

Led to be tempted, when the forty days
　Of that long Fast had run their weary
　　round,
There, face to face, to meet the Tempter's
　　gaze,
　And win the Victory on the well-fought
　　ground.

　　*　　*　　*　　*　　*

* "And was with the wild beasts."—S. Mark i. 13.

The struggle o'er,—swift from the Golden Gate
   A thousand Angel feet that desert trod,
And with adoring love around Him wait,—
   The Son of Mary and the Son of God!

We wander through the desert, still beset
   With sharp temptations and full many a snare ;
With tears of sorrow oft our eyes are wet,
   And scarce at times we falter forth our prayer.

Yet in the conflict—in each darkest hour,
   When storms sweep wildly o'er life's troubled sea,
When almost fainting 'neath the Tempter's power,
   Oh, suffering Jesus ! we will look to Thee !

And Thou wilt give us strength, and in Thy might
   We shall o'ercome, and in the "little while,"
Behold, in wonder, not the Angels' light,
   But, better far, Thine own approving smile.

" But now on Easter day when blessed spring
Hath flusht with beauty all the smiling land."—*Page* 75

EASTER DAY.

OW hard it was in dark November's gloom
    To join the high thanksgiving, as we
        stood
With throb of sorrow round that quiet
        tomb,
   "We bless Thee," O our Father wise and
        good !

It seemed so strange, with breaking hearts,
    to raise
    High o'er the " ashes and the dust to
        dust "
The chant of triumph and the song of praise,
    That told of surest hope and endless
        trust.

But now on Easter Day, when blessed Spring
    Hath flusht with beauty all the smiling
        land,
And hills and fruitful valleys laugh and sing
For all the bounties of her liberal hand,

We seem to scan with keener glance of faith,
  And deeper insight, life's strange mystery ;
To hear the " comfortable word " which saith,
  " How blest are they, in Jesus Christ, who die ! "

They only leave the long, sad earthly Lent,
    Oft dark with sorrow and oft dim with tears ;
They only strike with joy their desert tent,
    For the bright Home of the Eternal Years !

And Easter dawns for them,—a cloudless Day,
    Whose Sun of radiant splendour ne'er goes down :
They bore the Cross through all the desert way,
    And now they wear the Victor's fadeless Crown !

O Joy of Easter ! Light of endless Life,
    How sweet thy thoughts of solace are to me !
I hear the promise, through each bitter strife,
    That " where I am, there shall My servant be ! "

And so we thank Thee, Father, who in love
    Watchest with sleepless eye each burial sod ;
Our Easter light shall point to joys above,
    And the one Home of all the Sons of God !

THE LAST NIGHT OF THE OLD YEAR.

WATCHED the Old Year as it lay a-dying,
    The moon's cold light fell on the darkened
        bed,
I heard the winds their *Requiescat* sighing
    Over his weary head.

His work was done; and like a warrior
    olden,
    The hard fight o'er, he laid his armour
      down,
And passed all silent through the portal
    golden,
    Where gleams the victor's crown.

What a strange life it was! Oh, if the
    story
    Of all its joys and sorrows could be known,
How would dark shadows, mingling with its glory,
    Round its whole course be thrown!

How many tears have fallen hot and thickly;
    How many wounded hearts, with anguish sore,
Have uttered the deep longing, "O come quickly;
    Our buried hopes restore!"

E

How many blessed gifts of truest gladness
   His own dear Hand has scattered on our way !
How oft His voice of love amid our sadness,
      Turned darkness into day !

Old dying Year, thy memories are dearer
   Than any of thy grandsires gone before ;
I feel as though thy waves had brought me nearer
      To the Eternal Shore.

So here I bring its every sin and sorrow,
   Its deeds accomplished and its work undone,
To His dear Cross, and wait the bright to-morrow
      And the unsetting Sun.

Therefore, Old Year, farewell. I watch thee dying,
   Struggling in weakness for thy latest breath ;
I catch the lessons thou wouldst teach me, lying
      In the calm sleep of death.

And these thy last faint words, while morn doth brighten,—
   " Up and be doing ; lay in golden store ;
Till the great harvest of the world shall whiten,
      And Time shall be no more."

J. AND W. RIDER, PRINTERS, LONDON.